Coomacka Island:
The Story of Spider & Ant

Written by Don P. Hooper
Illustrated by Darnel Degand

Note for Librarians: A cataloguing record for this book is available from Library and Archives Canada at
www.collectionscanada.ca/amicus/index-e.html
ISBN 1-4120-9107-1

Printed in Victoria, BC, Canada. Printed on paper with minimum 30% recycled fibre.
Trafford's print shop runs on "green energy" from solar, wind and other environmentally-friendly power sources.

First Edition

Offices in Canada, USA, Ireland and UK

Book sales for North America and international:
Trafford Publishing, 6E–2333 Government St., Victoria, BC V8T 4P4 CANADA
phone 250 383 6864 (toll-free 1 888 232 4444)   fax 250 383 6804; email to orders@trafford.com
Book sales in Europe:
Trafford Publishing (UK) Limited, 9 Park End Street, 2nd Floor, Oxford, UK OX1 1HH UNITED KINGDOM
phone 44 (0)1865 722 113 (local rate 0845 230 9601)   facsimile 44 (0)1865 722 868; info.uk@trafford.com
Order online at: trafford.com/06-0863
For more information visit www.coomacka.com

10 9 8 7 6 5 4 3 2

FORWARD

About Coomacka Island

Coomacka Island is a mysterious uncharted island (meaning that you won't find this island on any map) in the Caribbean Sea. Four unlikely explorers stumbled on to this wondrous island while searching for the legendary Macka Tree. The Story of Spider & Ant is but one of many stories that the explorers documented on their travels through Coomacka Island.

We Understand that...

there are some words that may seem challenging to our audiences. Children who are read to typically have larger vocabularies and develop into proactive readers (don't take our word though; there are scientists upon scientists who will tell you the same). By age two, the average child can already recognize over 300 words. So we encourage you to speak and read to your children; expose them to new words through the dictionary and encyclopedia. It is never too early for your child to be immersed into the wonderful world of learning by reading. We assure you that they are up for the challenge.

At the end of this story, we have included a *Fun Activities & Words* section. There you will find a convenient glossary and questions from the book to share with your child.

Other Tales from Coomacka Island:
Anansi Jr. and the Mango Truck
Lenox Lizard and the Kukumacka Duppy

One morning, the thirsty Spider was exhausted from devouring the remainder of his water supply. Spider did not have the energy to travel to the nearest well, several miles away.

As always the cunning Spider had a brilliant idea. You see his friend the Ant would be stopping by shortly after noon, as he did everyday since childhood. Not only was Ant fast, he thought, but Ant also had several little brothers.

When Ant arrived, Spider convinced Ant that he had injured his leg when he caught Rat stealing his water last night.

Ant took pity on the injured Spider and got several of his brothers to help him rescue the water from the greedy Rat.

After bringing over forty buckets back, Ant asked the Spider if this was enough water. Spider urged Ant on by telling Ant that the drought may last for several months, and it would be best to get as much now as possible.

Late into the afternoon, Ant found himself exhausted. Despite the several hours of labor his family endured, Spider continued to urge them on.

When Ant saw one of his younger siblings fall from exhaustion, he decided it was time to tell Spider he was finished working for the day.

Ant found Spider's door locked, so he decided to go through the back entrance to avoid having Spider answer the door in his injured state.

As Ant began walking around Spider's house, he heard the faint sound of singing in the backyard.

Tip toeing closer, he saw the source of the voice. There was Spider in the backyard dancing and singing because he tricked the foolish Ant.

Ant left Spider's house upset; the sly Spider had tricked
Ant and his family.

Later that evening one of Ant's brothers went back to Spider's house. He told Spider that Ant passed out from the heat. The other ants were too little and weak to help bring their older brother back from the water well.

Spider, feeling guilty, went in search of Ant. He saw no trace of Ant along the path to the well.

Spider was very thirsty after the long journey, so he went to take a drink from the water well.

To his surprise there was no water left. The thirsty Spider searched one last time around the well for Ant.

As the sun set, Spider decided it was best to head home. Unfortunately, without light he was unable to find his way back home that night.

The frightened Spider was forced to spend the night alone in the forest.

The next day, when the sun had risen once again, Spider journeyed back home. When he arrived, he immediately went to his backyard to get a drink of water.

Spider was shocked to see that all the water buckets WERE GONE.

Ant and his brothers had taken the water back to the water well for all to enjoy.

Fun Activities & Words

I. Questions from *The Story of Spider & Ant*

1. Why did the Spider make up a story about the Rat stealing his water?

2. What caused the Spider to sing and dance?

3. The Spider was alone and afraid in the dark forest. What scares you? How can you overcome your fears?

4. The Spider took advantage of his friend the Ant. What could the Spider have done differently?

5. The Spider tried to keep all the water for himself. Why is it good to share?

II. Glossary

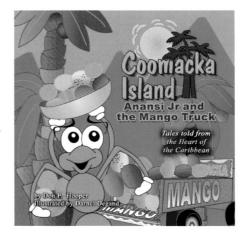

convinced (kuh n-vinsd)v. – to make someone agree
cunning (kuhn-ing)n. – sly, clever at tricking people
devouring (dǐ-vour)v. – to drink quickly and greedily
drought (drout)n. – dry weather, short supply of water
endured (en-dyoord)v. – to put up with patiently
entrance (en-truh-ns)n. – a doorway
exhausted (ig-zost-id)adj. – very tired
faint (feynt)adj. – low sounding
labor (ley-ber)n. – a job or task or work to be done
several (sev-ruhl)adj. – more than a few
siblings (sǐb'lǐngz) – brothers or sisters

Be sure to also check out:
*Coomacka Island: Anansi Jr.
and the Mango Truck*